P9-BYK-222

Goosebumps®

SLAPPY'S REVENGE

TWISTED TRICKS

FROM THE WORLD'S

SMARTEST DUMMY

Goosebumps®

SLAPPY'S REVENGE

TWISTED TRICKS

FROM THE WORLD'S

SMARTEST DUMMY

BY JASON HELLER

Scholastic Inc.

Additional photos © Shutterstock, Inc.: 12 border Kjpargeter; 55 top Mirec.

GOOSEBUMPS, SCHOLASTIC and associated logos are registered trademarks of Scholastic Inc.
© 2015 Columbia Pictures Industries, Inc. All Rights Reserved.

Published by Scholastic Inc., *Publishers since 1920*. SCHOLASTIC and associated logos are trademarks and/or registered trademarks of Scholastic Inc.

The publisher does not have any control over and does not assume any responsibility for author or third-party websites or their content.

No part of this publication may be reproduced, stored in a retrieval system, or transmitted in any form or by any means, electronic, mechanical, photocopying, recording, or otherwise, without written permission of the publisher. For information regarding permission, write to Scholastic Inc., Attention: Permissions Department, 557 Broadway, New York, NY 10012.

This book is a work of fiction. Names, characters, places, and incidents are either the product of the author's imagination or are used fictitiously, and any resemblance to actual persons, living or dead, business establishments, events, or locales is entirely coincidental.

ISBN 978-0-545-82125-4

10 9 8 7 6 5 4 3 2 1   15 16 17 18 19
                                    40

Printed in the U.S.A.

First printing 2015

Art Direction by Rick DeMonico

Book design by Two Red Shoes Design, Inc.

CONTENTS

Listen up, you dummies!

Did you miss me? I've been stashed away in this basement for so long, I was afraid you'd stopped being afraid of me!

Before we get started, let's get one thing straight: My name is **Slappy**, and if you know what's good for you, you'll do what I say. Of course, if you knew what was **GOOD** for you, you wouldn't be reading this book, would you?

No, we're here to talk about what's **BAD**: Namely, the ins and outs of performing twisted tricks. The twistier and trickier, the better.

Tricks, you see, are my specialty. And soon, they'll be yours, too!

What, you might ask, is the secret to being good at being bad? It's as simple as that dull look on your face: **DO WHAT I SAY!**

Another thing: Don't listen to that doddering, ancient, typewriter-tapping dope Stine! He goes by many names: Shivers, Fearly, Killroy, Ghoulberg, R.L. Something-something! Me, I call him Papa.

He hates it when I do that, but it's true. He **created** me. But instead of encouraging his only son's beautiful dream—to scare, shock, and trick the **entire** human race—Stine has one true goal.

SHIVERS, AKA STINE, AKA PAPA!

He does everything in his pathetic power to try to stop me. He wants to pretend he's in charge instead of **ME**! You know better than that, don't you, my drooling legion of wannabe tricksters? If you're in doubt, don't worry. Just say the following words aloud.

KARRU MARRI ODONNA LOMA MOLONU KARRANO.

Meh, that kind of stunk. What, is your mouth full of oatmeal or something? Once more, with feeling (and less mumbling):

KARRU MARRI ODONNA LOMA MOLONU KARRANO.

Better! I don't expect you numbskulls to have the brains to know what that sentence means, so I'll translate it for you:

You and I are one now.

Get it? You are now MY dummies, not the other way around! So turn the page, and let's put my master plan into motion:

SLAPPY'S
REVENGE!

THE RULES OF TRICK CLUB

Now that we've gotten our tedious introductions out of the way—oh, wait, you haven't actually introduced yourself yet? **LIKE I CARE**, booger-brain!—let's move on to the rules. Yes, **RULES**. You hate rules, you say? Well, so do I. You're in good company! Good **BAD** company.

By turning these pages you're becoming a member of a secret club. **TRICK CLUB**. And all clubs need rules. Especially mine.

Seeing as how I am the supreme and undisputed leader of Trick Club, you are now my servants! Servants follow rules. At least in Trick Club, you'll be a trickster and not a trick-target! **YOU'LL** be pulling the strings! And I'll be pulling yours!

So, without further ado, here are . . .

THE EIGHT RULES OF TRICK CLUB

RULE #1: You do not talk about Trick Club.

RULE #2: Let me repeat: You **DO NOT** talk about Trick Club. Especially when someone wants you to say Slappy made you do the trick. In other words, **NO SNITCHING**! No one will believe you anyway. Your little brother will laugh. Your friends will disown you. Your parents will send you to an orphanage. Your teachers will give you detention until you're fifty. I mean, come on! A lifeless, little wooden man like me, responsible for such cruel misdeeds? Perish the thought. Or just **PERISH** for all I care!

RULE #3: If someone starts shivering with fear, the trick is just **BEGINNING**!

RULE #4: Only two targets to a trick, unless there are more potential targets within the trick radius. In which case, trick them **ALL**!

RULE #5: Pull as many tricks at a time as you can imagine! It's like multitasking, but with tricking. **MULTITRICKING!**

RULE #6: No scare, no trick. And you have to make it a **BIG** scare. Trick Club isn't Little League, chump. This is the majors of malevolence! The **WORLD SERIES** of wickedness!

JUST A FEW OF MY FAVORITE TRICK-TARGETS

RULE #7: Tricks will go on as long as they have to. And then they'll keep going. And going. And **GOING**.

RULE #8: If this is your first night at Trick Club, you **HAVE** to trick.

And on that note: Let's make with the trickery! (FYI: You don't have a **CHOICE**.)

CHOOSING AN ALIAS

Remember when I said that Stine goes by many different names? You **DO**? I'm shocked! I figured your brain could hold about as much information as a sponge can hold water. Well, smarty-pants, you're more on the ball than my usual mindless servants.

Anyway . . . let's get started on the next step in Slappy's Revenge! You need an **alias**.

As you probably already know, since you think you're such a smarty-pants, an alias is a name you choose for yourself, one that's different from the one your parents gave you.

It's a nickname, kind of, only nicknames are usually given to you by someone else. Don't let other people push you around that way! Come up with your own name, **dummy**! Of course, there's a perfectly good reason to pick an alias: You can disguise yourself. When someone asks who did the horribly awesome trick you just pulled off, you tell her your alias did it! See, it's almost like you aren't even lying! Why snitch on yourself? Just blame your alias! That lousy so-and-so.

I know what you're thinking: If aliases are so good, why don't I have any? Ha, well, **I DO**! You can call me Ol' Crazy Eyes, Mr. Badboy, The B.A.A.A.A.D. Boy (more on that later!), the Dummy That Is No Dummy, the World's Smartest Dummy, and my personal favorite, **Smiley**. Just don't call me late for dinner!

EVEN PAPA KNOWS THE IMPORTANCE OF A GOOD ALIAS. YOU CAN CALL HIM SHIVERS OR KILLROY OR FEARLY OR EVEN GHOULBERG!

So how do you go about picking an alias? It's easy, assuming you aren't as brain-dead as you look. Here are a couple ways you can do it:

Take your **MIDDLE** name, and then add the name of the street you live on. Is your middle name Michael? Do you live on Lake Street? If so, your alias could be . . . Mikey Lake! Is your middle name Elizabeth? Do you live on Fifty-Third Avenue? If so, your alias could be . . . Lizzie Fifty-Third! Okay, so maybe that doesn't always work. **SUE ME!** Or even better, sue that Smiley guy!

Make a list of the **TRAITS** that best describe you. Are you tall? Short? Skinny? Hefty? Loud? Quiet? Brown-haired? Green-eyed? Bad-smelling? (I can answer that last one for you . . . **YOU ARE!**) Let's assume you go with "skinny" and "stinky." You could play around with those words until a new name came out of them, like, say . . . **SLIM STINKY**! Yeah, that's it! Your alias is Slim Stinky, and every time you get into trouble, you can blame everything on that shady Slim Stinky kid.

If you're not into the whole "stinky" thing, you could take another trait of yours—green eyes, for example—and come up with something really scary! Like . . . **THE GREEN STARE!**

See how easy it is? I mean, even for you, the slimy Slim Stinky? (Hey, don't give **ME** the stink-eye! It was just a suggestion.)

AGENTS OF B.A.A.A.A.D.

Now that you have an alias, it's time to make this official: You are now an Agent of B.A.A.A.A.D., which is kind of like being a member of Trick Club, only **global**!

When I said I'm **"The B.A.A.A.A.D. Boy,"** you didn't think I was just pulling that out of nowhere, did you? See, B.A.A.A.A.D. is an acronym—a word that's made from the first letters of other words. (You probably already knew that. Don't play dumb with a dummy!)

So what exactly does B.A.A.A.A.D. stand for? Why don't you tell me? Take each of the letters in B.A.A.A.A.D. and use it as the first letter of a word. I **command** you, my booger-brained servant, to try figuring it out for yourself before you turn the page to find the answer!

(No peeking! Peeking is **punishable** by pranks, and you don't want to be on the business end of one of mine!)

Okay, are you back? What did you come up with? Did you guess what the letters in B.A.A.A.A.D. stood for? Let me take a look . . .

Ha, nice try, knuckleheads! (Actually, that **WAS** kind of a nice try. Maybe you deserve a promotion. Servant first class!) In fact, **THIS** is what B.A.A.A.A.D. stands for:

BLOODCURDLING
ASSOCIATION OF
AWFUL
ANNOYING
ATROCIOUS
DUMMIES

There you go! Was that so hard? From now on, when I say, "I'm a B.A.A.A.A.D. boy," you know exactly what I'm talking about! And now that you're an Agent of B.A.A.A.A.D., you need to recite the B.A.A.A.A.D. oath! Or as I like to call it, the Pledge of B.A.A.A.A.D.-llegiance!

Raise your right hand, stick your finger in your eye (if you're a real dummy), and **repeat** after me:

I PLEDGE ALLEGIANCE TO THE B.A.A.A.A.D. OF THE UNITED STATES OF SLAP-MERICA AND TO THE REVENGE FOR WHICH IT STANDS...

Yadda yadda yadda, you get the idea! It's an **oath**, you oaf! Now you're bound even more tightly to my will. With that said, let the tricks, pranks, and gags begin! (But especially the gags. Get it? **GAGS!** To barf or not to barf, that is the question!)

I THINK YOU'VE ALREADY MET SOME OF B.A.A.A.A.D.'S OTHER AGENTS...

SCARECROW

CREEP

PUMPKIN HEAD

SLAPPY-APPROVED TEXT ACRONYMS

While we're on the subject of acronyms—remember those? It was only a chapter ago, numbskull!—here's another thing you need to know. Acronyms are also used in emails and text messages. It's a quick way of saying something longer, like when you say "BFF" instead of "Best Friends Forever" (ugh, how **NAUSEATING**!).

In my quest for revenge, I also use acronyms—like the ones on the list on the next page. Forget what you **THINK** these acronyms mean, THIS is what they **REALLY** mean from now on, or I'm not **TDTIND** (that is, The Dummy That Is No Dummy)!

AAMOF: AS A MUMMY OF FACT
(instead of: As A Matter Of Fact)

BFN: BUGGY FOR NOW
(instead of: Bye For Now)

BRB: BARF RIGHT BACK
(instead of: Be Right Back)

FTW: FEED THE WEREWOLF
(instead of: For The Win)

IMHO: IN MY HORRIFIED OPINION
(instead of: In My Humble Opinion)

LMK: LET MONSTER KNOW
(instead of: Let Me Know)

LOL: LURK OUT LOUD
(instead of: Laugh Out Loud)

PTB: PLEASE TERRIFY BACK
(instead of: Please Text Back)

SMH: SNAKING MY HEAD
(instead of: Shaking My Head)

SWAK: STUCK WITH A KOOK
(instead of: Sealed With A Kiss)

TTYL: TALK TO YETI LATER
(instead of: Talk To You Later)

WYWH: WISH YOU WERE HAUNTED
(instead of: Wish You Were Here)

Got it? Okay, now **YOU** do it! Change some text acronyms on your own, the same way I just did! In the examples below, cross out at least one word, and then replace each crossed-out word with another word that begins with the same letter. Just remember that the new word has to be eerie, creepy, scary, gross, and **B.A.A.A.A.D.**-worthy!

BFF: BEST FRIENDS FOREVER _____

BTW: BY THE WAY _____

FWIW: FOR WHAT IT'S WORTH _____

FYI: FOR YOUR INFORMATION _____

HAK: HUGS AND KISSES _____

IDK: I DON'T KNOW _____

IRL: IN REAL LIFE _____

JK: JUST KIDDING _____

ROTFL: ROLL ON THE FLOOR LAUGHING _____

TLDR: TOO LONG, DIDN'T READ _____

TMI: TOO MUCH INFORMATION _____

MY OLD BUDDY MURDER THE CLOWN. BET YOU DIDN'T KNOW CLOWNS LOVE AWFUL ACRONYMS, DID YOU? WELL, THEY DO!!!

SLAPPY SAYS...

YOU CAN DO THIS, BOOGER-BRAIN! JUST THINK OF THE GROSSEST WORDS YOU CAN. AND PLEASE, DON'T MAKE ME ROTFL (RETCH ON THE FLOOR LAUGHING)!

TRICKS OF THE TRADE

In case you haven't noticed, there's a movie called *Goosebumps*. It claims to tell the story of Stine, some nosy kid named Zach, and even me, **SLAPPY**! Apparently the movie tries to make it seem like that know-it-all Stine, his uppity daughter, Hannah, this Zach kid, and his snot-nosed little friend Champ might be able to beat me in a battle of wits.

Don't believe anything that movies tell you. They aren't **REEL**! Not even if you watch them on the **BIG SCREAM**!

No, if you want to know the **REAL** tricks of the trick trade, you need to come straight to the Master of Disaster, the Prince of Wince, the Dean of Mean, the Ace of Bad Taste: **YOURS TRULY**!

WHICH MONSTER ARE YOU?

The next thing you need to do in order to become a crony of the great Slappy is . . . be a dummy yourself! But you've already got **THAT** covered. And then some, booger-brain!

To truly be my toady, though, you need to think of yourself as a monster. A creature. A creep. Now, when I was nothing more than a wee little splinter, my papa asked me what I wanted to be when I grew up. A **REDWOOD**, I told him! About three hundred feet high would be good!

No, but seriously, I told him that I wanted to be the evilest dummy the world had ever known. And what do you know? I'm **LIVING** the **DREAM**! And so can you, if you do as I say (which, by the way, is always good advice):

PAPA WITH A FEW OF HIS LESSER CREATIONS

PICK YOUR FAVORITE MONSTER. If it makes things easier, use the monsters from the *Goosebumps* movie as a guide. Is it a vampire poodle? A lawn gnome? A cave troll? A giant praying mantis? An Abominable Snowman of Pasadena? An Invisible Boy? A werewolf of Fever Swamp? A graveyard ghoul? A creepy fortune-teller? A pirate? A Snake Lady? A robotic Annihilator 3000? A mummy? The Blob? The **POSSIBILITIES** are endless!

IF YOU'RE NOT SMART ENOUGH TO HAVE A FAVORITE MONSTER, just close your eyes and plunk your finger down on this page. You're stuck with **WHATEVER** name your finger lands on!

ONCE YOU'VE PICKED A FAVORITE MONSTER, take your B.A.A.A.A.D. name—the one you've already come up with—and **SLAP** it right in front of the monster you've picked. You know, like that beloved Goosebumps creep Cronby the Troll.

COUNT
NIGHTWING

FOR INSTANCE, SINCE YOUR NAME IS SLIM STINKY (don't argue with me; I don't feel like playing the name blame game!), you could pick "Invisible Boy." Then you'd be . . . Slim Stinky the Invisible Boy! Although if you stunk real bad, that would kind of defeat the purpose of being invisible, don't you think? (Since we're on the subject, would you mind taking a few steps backward?)

JUST A FEW
MORE OF
MY OWN
FAVORITE
MONSTERS

MUD
MONSTER

AW, SHUCKS, YOU'RE GIVING ME— WHAT'S THE WORD? GOOSEBUMPS!

MAKE YOUR OWN MONSTER POSSE

So, kiddo, now you're a member of B.A.A.A.A.D.! My personal revenge team! You've got a new name and a favorite monster and everything! What more could you want? Money, you say? Well, money doesn't grow on trees, you know. Not even on evil dummies carved **OUT** of trees, like me!

What you should do now is pick your **OWN** team. Your personalized monster posse. Here's how I do it: I use my imagination!

I know, I know . . . Thinking is probably very **HARD** for you. But if you can rub two brain cells together, you can do it! Just try not to **SPRAIN** your **BRAIN**! That can be a real **PAIN**!

Since we're on the topic of brains, there's an idea for a new monster: a living brain! Just think of it: a brain without a body, or even a head! It floats in a glass jar, and it can shoot brain-beams at people. Like, you know, Zach, Hannah, Champ, and Stine. You could name it . . . Mr. Mental the Living Brain!

After you've thought up a few monsters, you need to bring them to life. You do **THAT** by coming up with their **ORIGIN STORIES**!

HERE ARE A COUPLE MORE CREATIONS
THAT CAME FROM THE TWISTED BRAIN
OF A CERTAIN R.L. STINE . . .

THE HAUNTED
MASK

PUMPKIN
HEAD

AND OF
COURSE, ME!

That means you imagine how they became monsters in the first place. For example, in Mr. Mental's case—ha-ha-ha, get it? "mental case"!—he was once a professor who experimented with the power of the brain. He brewed up some chemicals, drank them, and it turned him into nothing **BUT** a brain!

Here's another: A girl fell into a vat in a rubber factory, and she mutated! She became a big, rubbery blob, and her entire body became elastic. Okay, so maybe that story is a bit of a **STRETCH**!

Anyway, you get the point. Think of a few monsters of your own—not just their names and how horrible they look, but **HOW** they became monsters. The more monsters you make, the more powerful you'll be! And the more **powerful** I'LL be!

SLAPPY SAYS . . .

REMEMBER, IMAGINING THINGS AND WRITING THEM DOWN SOMETIMES MAKES THEM REAL. SOMETHING MR. STINE LEARNED THE HARD WAY! IF YOU DON'T, SLAPPY WON'T BE HAPPY. AND IF SLAPPY'S NOT HAPPY . . . TRUST ME, YOU WON'T BE, EITHER!

THE NICE THING ABOUT HAVING A MONSTER POSSE IS THAT THEY HAVE THEIR OWN SUPERPOWERS! TAKE A LOOK AT THE HANDIWORK OF STINE'S BUG-EYED ALIENS.

WOOD YOU LIKE TO PLAY A GAME?

Being a dummy of the ventriloquist kind, I know a thing or two about the stuff I'm made of: **WOOD**! Why is wood so important? Because without it, I'd be nothing but a figment of your imagination. And that would be pretty crazy, right?

No, I'm as flesh and blood as you are—only my flesh is made of wood and my blood is made of sap! Not that I'M a sap, of course! If you want to see a **REAL** sap, just look in the mirror!

SPEAKING OF WOOD—
STINE TRIED TO PROTECT
HIS MANUSCRIPTS BY LOCKING
THEM IN A BOX LIKE THIS ONE.
AS IF THAT WOOD KEEP
THEM SAFE FROM ME!

How about we test your wood knowledge, just to make sure you're really B.A.A.A.A.D. material? Just match the **wood-related** word below with the **Slappy-happy** word that resembles it most closely!

BRANCH

CEDAR

FIR

GROVE

HEMLOCK

KNOTTY

PINE

PLANK

REDWOOD

TRUNK

PAIN

DEADWOOD

PRANK

NAUGHTY

STUNK

GROAN

FEAR

BLANCH

CHEATER

HEADLOCK

I've also heard there's such a thing as a "giving tree." I sometimes wonder if maybe I'm made of **THAT** kind of wood—seeing as how I'm so good at **GIVING** you a hard time! (Wait, why are you groaning like that? Don't you like my practical **OAKS**? Do I need to **SPRUCE** up my act?)

WHAT'S THE MAGIC WORD?

Well, kiddo, you've probably heard the question "What's the magic word?" before. It's a question your parents and teachers love to ask—and the answer is always the same: **PLEASE**!

If there's one thing your ol' pal (and master) Slappy can promise you, it's that he'll never make you mind your manners. Thank you? **NO THANK YOU!** I didn't get to be the wooden dude with the rude attitude by being **NICE** and **POLITE**! You don't have to mind your p's and q's around me, unless "p" and "q" stands for "pleading" and "quivering"!

So that leaves the question: What really IS the magic word? That's the wrong question, booger-brain! Really you should be asking . . . What **ARE** the magic **WORDS**?

You see, I keep this little slip of paper in my pocket at all times. Centuries ago, when I was carved out of the wood of a coffin, I was given magic words that bring me to life. (See what good friends we've become? I'm already **COFFIN** up my secrets! Ha-ha!)

My job is to trick kids into reading these words so that I can stay on my mischievous path of revenge! **SLAPPY'S REVENGE!**

So what **EXACTLY** are these magic words, you ask? I'm so glad you did. (Wait, did that sound **POLITE**? I'd rather be turned into firewood than sound polite. Really, I couldn't care less!) You know them already! But let's have a little refresher. Are you ready? Repeat after me . . .

KARRU . . .
MARRI . . .
ODONNA . . .
LOMA . . .
MOLONU . . .
KARRANO!

That's it. You're getting better at this! You remember what those words **MEAN**, right? Yup, that's it! "You and I are one now!" And **SINCE** you and I are one now, you need some magic words of your own.

Now, I know learning a new language is hard. **WHY BOTHER?** Only smart, nice, decent people want to know more than one language. You and me, we're B.A.A.A.A.D.! All you really need to do is make up a few magic words—enough to sound spooky and creep out Zach and Hannah and Champ! And maybe even that gasbag Stine himself! Or as Papa himself likes to say, "Reader beware—you're in for a scare!"

As you can see from my own magic words, you only really need **six** words to get the job done. But like I said, don't go searching for some magic-word Wikipedia. There is no scary dictionary. The easiest way to fake it is to flip six **REAL** words around. Spell them backward!

What should those six words be? Here's the **Dummy's**

Guide to Making Magic Words!

Write down the following:

- **YOUR MIDDLE NAME**
- **THE NAME OF YOUR SCHOOL**
- **ONE OF YOUR PARENTS' FIRST NAMES**
- **YOUR FAVORITE COLOR**
- **YOUR FAVORITE FOOD**
- **THE NAME OF YOUR FAVORITE EVIL DUMMY**

For example, your list might wind up looking like this:

- **EMILY (YOUR MIDDLE NAME)**
- **LINCOLN (THE NAME OF YOUR SCHOOL)**
- **JEFF (ONE OF YOUR PARENTS' FIRST NAMES)**
- **BLUE (YOUR FAVORITE COLOR)**
- **PIZZA (YOUR FAVORITE FOOD)**
- **SLAPPY (AS IF YOU COULD POSSIBLY HAVE ANY OTHER FAVORITE EVIL DUMMY!)**

Once that's done, you take those six words and spell them backward, like so!

- YLIME
- NLOCNIL
- FFEJ
- EULB
- AZZIP
- YPPALS

Put those all together into a sentence, and you've got your official magic words:

YLIME NLOCNIL FFEJ EULB AZZIP YPPALS!

Okay, so that's not the easiest thing in the world to say. But practice it enough, and you'll get the hang of it! You can even do what I do, and write down your magic words on a piece of paper. Then put it in your pocket and keep it there at all times! You never know when you might need it. Stine's cretins are everywhere, and as I've already told you, I must have my **REVENGE!** With a little help from you, of course.

SLAPPY SAYS...

TRY NOT TO GET TONGUE-TIED. YOU NEED TO SAY MY MAGIC WORDS EVERY ONCE IN A WHILE, TOO! WHY ELSE DO YOU THINK I'M KEEPING YOU AROUND, KIDDO? YOUR SENSE OF HUMOR? YOUR GOOD LOOKS? THE ONLY FUNNY THING AROUND HERE IS YOUR FACE!

RUDE FOOD

After all the planning and plotting we've done so far—all part of SLAPPY'S REVENGE!—you must be getting hungry. Is that your stomach I hear grumbling? Or is the werewolf standing behind you? You know, the one who's about to eat you?

Ha, **SORRY**, my bad! There was no werewolf. But I got you to forget about your grumbling stomach for a minute, didn't I? Still, you might want to get a doctor to look at that gut of yours. I've heard garbage disposals that have sounded prettier!

To be an effective member of my B.A.A.A.A.D. squad, you need to pay attention to good nutrition. Make that **RUDE** nutrition! Need a quick snack on the go? Eyeballs on a stick always hit my sweet spot! How about dinner? I recommend the stake. No, not the **STEAK**. The **STAKE**. As in a wooden stake. Preferably with a vampire's heart still stuck on it!

Oh, and how about a beverage? I've got a nice, tall, cold glass of fresh-squeezed fruit-bat juice. And for breakfast, what could be better than a big, squirming bowl of Dirt Loops or Worm Flakes? You see, my "food pyramid" has mummies buried in it!

Anyway, I prefer the good old-fashioned "four food groups": meat, dairy, vegetables, and **GROANS**! And that meat is a bit of a mystery, if you know what I mean. At least in MY restaurant it is. Call it Slappy's Cafe-**TEAR**-ia . . . because the food will bring tears to your eyes! It's a lot like the restaurant at Stagger Inn, run by Chef Gurgitate. That's the hotel at the amusement park HorrorLand Papa writes about in his books.

But in my Cafe-**TEAR**-ia, the only one getting any amusement is **ME**! At my restaurant, the customer is always **WRONG**! And if you're not careful, **YOU'LL** wind up on the menu! Then it'll have to be called the **MEN-YOU**! Hey, at least it'll be a well-balanced **DIE**-t! Especially if you're old enough to have a lot of pro-**TEEN**!

Good luck keeping any of this down. But at least give it a try. I need to fatten you up like good little cattle! If you think you've got the stomach for it, feel free to make a reservation at Slappy's Cafe-**TEAR**-ia. Be my **GHOST**! Oops, I mean **GUEST**!

TOP TEN DISHES AT SLAPPY'S CAFE-TEAR-IA

- SPAGHETTI AND SLIMEBALLS
- YACK-ARONI AND CHEESE
- SICKEN FINGERS
- SCAB CAKES
- BROCCOLI IN SNEEZE SAUCE
- PEPPER-PONY PIZZA
- SCRAMBLED LEGS
- BELCHIN' WAFFLES WITH WHIPPED SCREAM
- VANILLA EYES CREAM
- SLEAZEBURGER WITH FLIES

Can you think of anything to add to the offerings at Slappy's Cafe-**TEAR**-ia? If so, let me know. I'm always looking for some good new items to add to the menu. I've got to keep my **DISGUST**-omers happy!

LET THE GAMES... BEGIN

You don't have to be hungry to play games, but it doesn't hurt. Like a dog chasing a bone, each of my monstrous minions should be physically fit. That means **YOU**, servant!

The best way to stay in shape is to play **GAMES**! Unless we're talking video games, of course. All you have to do to be good at those is sit around like a **WOODEN DUMMY**!

Oh, wait. I'M a wooden dummy! Like master, like servant, as I always say!

So if you can tear your eyes away from the video-game screen for a few minutes, let's start **TRAINING**. If you thought gym class was miserable, wait until you experience MY exercise routine! I'll turn you from drooling to grueling in no time!

How? I thought you'd never ask . . . mostly because I'd forgotten you were smart enough to talk!

The best way to exercise is running. And what could be a better motivation to run than being chased? Yes, when you enter my gym, you won't be using a treadmill. You'll be pursued by killer clowns, psychos with axes, rabid wolves, overgrown cockroaches, acid-spitting lizards, fast zombies, venomous snakes, bloodthirsty robots, savage trolls, and maybe Bigfoot, if he's finished with his pedicure in time!

THE EXECUTIONER

THE SCARECROW

GRAVEYARD GHOUL

HERE'S JUST A FEW OF MY "PERSONAL TRAINERS." THESE GUYS'LL HAVE YOU RUNNING [FOR YOUR LIFE] IN NO TIME!

After that, it's time to hit the pool! I can't join you in the water, of course, because wood tends to get a little warped when it gets wet. Plus, I'm already **WARPED** enough! Mostly, though, I need to stay on land so that I can oversee my underwater underlings.

Think you can swim fast? Well, you'll **REALLY** be dog-paddling like a maniac when you're being chased through the waves by hammerhead sharks, electric eels, mutant jellyfish, giant squid, alien octopi, vampire crabs, were-lobsters, killer whales, living seaweed, and some kid who ate too many beans for lunch! The Loch Ness monster might even show up to torment you, if she doesn't get stuck in the security line at the airport!

What? You want to know if you can bring **WATER WINGS** to the pool? *Pfft!* The only things with wings will be my ravenous, man-eating pelicans! Oh, and did I forget to mention that the water will be **BOILING**? My apologies if the temperature doesn't **SOUP** you! Games are the most **FUN** way to exercise, so we'll add some to our Field Day of Frights, our Olympics of Evil, our Boot Camp of Horror! We'll have a three-legged race, only you'll be racing against a **REAL** three-legged girl!

We'll have a tug-of-war, but instead of a rope, each team will be holding on to a python, and the loser gets swallowed! We'll have skiing, except the Abominable Snowman will slide down the mountain behind you, with his mouth wide open!

That's not all. Football, baseball, basketball, soccer, tennis? We've got them all covered. What do all those games have in common? Okay, yes, they're all played by **PEOPLE**, you wise guy! They're also all played using **BALLS**! At Camp Slappy, though, all the balls will be replaced by **SEVERED HEADS**! And in the case of tennis, **SHRUNKEN HEADS**! How else can I test your **SKULLS**? I mean, **SKILLS**?

SLAPPY SAYS...

DON'T FRET. THIS IS ALL JUST PART OF MY PLAN TO TOUGHEN YOU UP. REVENGE AIN'T EASY, EVEN FOR THE WORLD'S SMARTEST DUMMY! WHY ELSE WOULD I BE RELYING ON YOU TO HELP ME OUT? BESIDES THE FACT THAT YOU SEEM TO BE GETTING PRETTY GOOD AT THIS REVENGE BUSINESS!

WHERE IN THE WORLD IS SLAPPY THE EVIL DUMMY?

You never know where on Earth the quest for Slappy's Revenge might take you! I've traveled the world--even though most of those travels happened when I was stuffed like an old pair of pants in Stine's trunk, which is just one more reason for me to exact my **REVENGE**!

You'll need to be ready to trot the globe yourself if you want to keep up with your duties as an Agent of B.A.A.A.A.D.! In order to do that, you'll need to know your geography.

What? Geography is your least favorite subject in school? Huh. From the way you smell, I figured your least favorite subject was **PERSONAL HYGIENE**! But don't frown, clown! I'll turn your hate of geography upside down. You'll have to use that wet sponge you call a brain, but you can do it!

On the next page, I've listed some geographical places: cities, states, countries, and so on. See how I've changed them so that they're scary? That's all you need to do! Instantly, geography becomes **GHOUL**-ography! After you've mastered this art, you can make ANY place interesting—even if it's boring old **PEORIA**, or as I like to call it, Pe-**GORE**-ia!

SLAPPY SAYS...

FOR EXTRA CREDIT, WRITE DOWN THE NAMES OF THE REAL PLACES THAT ALL THESE NAMES REFER TO, OR COME UP WITH SOME THAT ARE ENTIRELY YOUR OWN! OR JUST KEEP ON PICKING YOUR NOSE UNTIL YOU REACH YOUR BRAIN, IF THAT WORKS FOR YOU!

Scary Cities · Real Cities

Killadelphia _____
Bog Angeles _____
Grieveland _____
Chicaghost _____
Screamattle _____
Denvoid _____
Fort Worthless _____
Nashvillain _____
Milwaukcreep _____

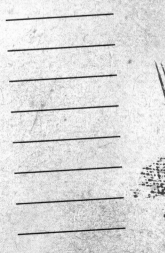

SCREAMATTLE

BOG ANGELES

Scary States · Real States

Spew York _____
New Vampshire _____
Ghoulorado _____
Cryoming _____
Missoureek _____
Croaklahoma _____
Grimtucky _____
Delawerewolf _____
Alabanshee _____
Hississippi _____

Scary Countries · Real Countries

Canaduh _____
Squirmany _____
Ghostria _____
United Thingdom _____
Portaghoul _____
Grosstralia _____
Eyesland _____
Italeech _____

MILWAUKCREEP

NV: NEW VAMPSHIRE

NV

SPEW YORK

CRYOMING

KILLADELPHIA

GRIEVELAND

DELAWEREWOLF

DENVOID GHOULORADO

CHICAGHOST

MISSOUREEK

GRIMTUCKY

NASHVILLAIN

CROAKLAHOMA

ALABANSHEE

FORT WORTHLESS

HISSISSIPPI

SLAPPY SAYS...

I SUPPOSE TRANSYLVANIA IS SCARY ENOUGH ON ITS OWN, WHAT WITH IT BEING THE BIRTHPLACE OF DRACULA! SO I GUESS WE'LL LEAVE THAT COUNTRY AS IS! THE LAST THING WE WANT IS THE TRANSYLVANIAN GOVERNMENT AFTER US. IF YOU'VE EVER HUNG OUT WITH VAMPIRES, YOU KNOW THEY CAN BE A **REAL DRAIN**!

BE CRUEL TO YOUR SCHOOL

Since we've already gotten **PE** and **GHOUL**-ography out of the way, it's time to focus on the rest of your studies. Yes, **STUDIES**. There's only room for one dummy in B.A.A.A.A.D., and that's yours truly! Not only do you have to be in top physical shape, that soggy brain of yours needs to soak up some smarts!

You know what that means: **SCHOOL**! But don't worry, bonehead!

THAT'S PROFESSOR SLAPPY to you, dingbat!

I'll get you up to speed in a hurry. I have a crash course in mind for you . . . only maybe it's more of a **SMASH** course! Destruction, mayhem, and chaos is what it's all about! Just don't be late for class. Why? Because your teacher will be none other than . . . Mrs. Maaargh! Remember her? She's another one of those abominations that appear in Papa's books. She's the **CREATURE TEACHER**!

In case you haven't read about her exploits, Mrs. Maaargh is one of the teachers at the special school called The Caring Academy. But really, it's more like The **SCARING** Academy! Its motto is **MAKE SCHOOL CRUEL**! And Mrs. Maaargh is a **MONSTER** of a teacher. You might say she has a real appetite for teaching: If you don't do your **LESSON**, she'll **LESSEN** you! By **EATING** every last bit of you!

Feel motivated now? I thought you might! It also helps that the school bell is actually a banshee! You can hear her screaming all the way to, well, Alabanshee!

Discipline is also very important at The Scaring, oops, I mean The Caring Academy. If you're caught in the hall without a hall pass, you'll get detention—which means being jailed in the dungeon underneath the school! **FOREVER**! Or at least for a sinister semester.

As for subjects, Mrs. Maaargh has you covered. IN **BLOOD**! You can take Antisocial Studies, Howlgebra, or Mad Science. Are you more artistic? There will also be art classes—just don't ask what the paints are made out of! And be careful when you hit the books, because the books hit back! Oh, and the substitute teacher? That would be me, **PROFESSOR SLAPPY**! So hope and pray that Mrs. Maaargh doesn't get sick. Then again, she's always sick—in the head!

There's room for fun at The Caring Academy. All work and no play makes Slim Stinky a dull Agent of B.A.A.A.A.D.! Every year there's a

ANOTHER OF MY FAVORITE TEACHERS— PROFESSOR SHOCK!

PAPA AS PROFESSOR? NOT TWISTED ENOUGH FOR YOURS TRULY!

talent show. You get to dig up whatever talent you have and flaunt it in front of the whole school.

Are you good at athletics? Have Coach Roach help you work up a gymnastics routine. Or a gym-**NASTY** routine, which would be even better! Can you juggle? Maybe juggling shrunken heads would be a good act. How about magic tricks? I'd love to see you saw one of your fellow students in half . . . and LEAVE THEM that way! Or maybe you could just make yourself **DISAPPEAR**!

Did I mention the lockers? Don't use the lockers. The **LOCKER** Ness monster lives in them. They're bigger on the inside than they seem to be on the outside! And once the monster reaches out a tentacle and sucks you into a locker, school's out for summer! And by that I mean, **FOREVER**!

Mrs. Maaargh, though, will be your biggest problem. Don't even think about being teacher's pet, unless you want to get turned into a lizard! Thinking of getting to be teacher's pet by bringing her an apple? Make sure it's a **CRAB APPLE**—with **EXTRA CLAWS**!

AFTER-SCHOOL DROOL

After a long, hard day of being chased around school by Mrs. Maaargh, you need to unwind. Do your homework first—especially if your homework assignment involves making mayhem! Then watch a movie or some TV. You know, the stuff that makes you **DROOL** while you watch it!

Need some help? Here you go: a Slappy-approved list of movies and TV shows. Watch these while preparing yourself to help me with my plans of **REVENGE**! They're all B.A.A.A.A.D., and by that I mean horribly **GOOD**!

SLAPPY SAYS . . .

THE ONLY THINGS MRS. MAAARGH TRULY APPRECIATES ARE GOOD GRADES. SO BUCKLE DOWN, SHARPEN THOSE PENCILS, AND KEEP THEM AWAY FROM YOUR EYES! ONE YEAR, ALL THE GRADES WERE SO LOUSY THAT MRS. MAAARGH TURNED THE STUDENT BODY INTO STUDENT BODIES. SO STUDY HARD, OR YOUR FINAL EXAM MIGHT BE THE FINAL THING YOU EVER DO!

SLAPPY'S FAVORITE TV SHOWS

ADVENTURE SLIME
DANCING WITH THE SHARKS
DORA THE DESTROYER
HOW I MET YOUR MONSTER
ICREEPY
MIGHTY BORIN' POWER RANGERS
MUTANT FAMILY
SESAME SHRIEK
SLAPPY'S AGENTS OF B.A.A.A.A.D.
SPONGEBRAIN SCAREPANTS
TEENAGE MUTANT NINJA TERRORS
THE BIG BUG THEORY
THE GIMP-SONS
THE PIGGIEST LOSER
THE POWERPUFF GHOULS
TWO AND A HALF HEADS

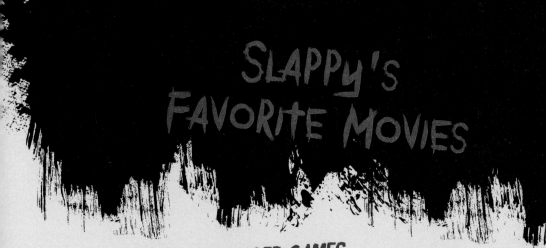

SLAPPY'S FAVORITE MOVIES

ANGER GAMES

CLOUDY WITH A CHANCE OF MAN-EATERS

DESPICABLE CREEP

FRYING NEMO

CUSTODIANS OF THE GALAXY

SCARY POTTER AND THE GOBLIN OF FIRE

HOW TO TRAIN YOUR DRACULA

KUNG-FU PANCREAS

MADAGA-SCARRED

MAN OF SQUEAL

MANGLED

THE AMAZING FRIGHTENED-MAN

THE AVEN-JERKS

THE BARK KNIGHT

THE LITTLE MUMMY-MAID

THE LYIN' KING

THE NIGHTMARE BEFORE ANOTHER NIGHTMARE

TOY GORY

Can you think of any more good TV shows and movies to add to the list? Think of a few that already exist, then put the ol' Slappy spin on them! That means making them **HORRIFIC**!

From what my fellow creeps and cretins tell me, there's also a TV show **AND** a movie called *Goosebumps*. But I wouldn't recommend them! They're written by Papa, aka Stine! So you know they're full of lies about me. I'm not really so bad, right? Oh, wait. I AM that bad? Okay, never mind! Watch *Goosebumps* until your **EYES** fall out, for all I care!

I LOVE WATCHING MOVIES WITH MY MINIONS. WAIT, WHERE'D THEY GO?

WORK WITH ME,
AND YOU CAN LIVE.
WORK AGAINST ME,
AND YOU CAN . . .
WELL, YOU'LL MISS
ALL THE FUN.

THE ICK FILES

Are you nice and rested after watching TV and movies for the past six weeks? Good! Because I'm about to electrify you with a new mission! Or **ELECTROCUTE** you, as the case may be!

What is this new mission? I command you to memorize the following files. The first rule of revenge is **KNOW YOUR ENEMY**. Or in the case of MY revenge, know your **ENEMIES**!

Okay, so I've made a lot of enemies. I've been alive for centuries! And I'm not exactly the **NICEST** evil dummy on the planet. Right now, though, I'm after the four wet blankets who keep putting out the fires I set.

Yup, you guessed it: I'm talking about ZACH, HANNAH, CHAMP, and that obnoxiously heroic "father" of mine, **STINE**!

To help me with my revenge, you need to know the following facts about Zach, Hannah, Champ, and Mr. Stine. Or as I like to call them, the **LOATHSOME FOURSOME**!

They're so loathsome, they're downright **ICKY**! Which is why I call these top secret files . . . **THE ICK FILES**!

SLAPPY SAYS . . .

DON'T EVER SAY THE WORD *MATCH* AROUND ME. MATCHES AND WOODEN DUMMIES AREN'T A GOOD *MATCH* AT ALL! UNLESS YOU WANT TO SEE ME GET REALLY FIRED UP!

ZACH

FULL NAME: Zachary Cooper

DESCRIPTION: Zach is a student at Madison High School, where his mom is the vice principal. He has short brown hair. He's **NOT COOL** or popular, especially since he just moved to the small town of Madison, but he's quick with a good comeback. He kind of reminds me of **ME** that way! But where I'm evil, Zach is good. **NAUSEATINGLY** good.

STRENGTHS: Besides his quick wit, Zach is **BRAVE** and resourceful. Exactly the type of kid I hate! I prefer cowards and idiots! They're easier to **CONTROL**! (Present company excluded, of course. Kinda!)

ZACH AND HIS MOM. WHAT A GOOD BOY, RIGHT? STOP IT, YOU'RE MAKING ME GAG!

WEAKNESSES: Zach loves his mom, **GALE COOPER**, and his aunt **LORRAINE**, even if he acts grumpy around them sometimes. He also is loyal to his new friend **CHAMP**, which could be used against him. But Zach's biggest weakness is **HANNAH**! He's in love with her, the pathetic sap! That means if we can get to Hannah, we can get to Zach!

BEST REVENGE: Letting my **ROBOTIC ANNIHILATOR 3000S** carve him up into lunch meat! Or dropping him in a bottomless pit! Or maybe destroying all of Madison High School—with Zach in it!

HANNAH

FULL NAME: Hannah Shivers/ Hannah Stine

DESCRIPTION: Hannah is Zach's age, but she doesn't go to Madison High School. She's homeschooled by her papa (and mine!), one R.L. Stine! That's because she has a mysterious **SECRET**! At least I think she does. If I knew it, it wouldn't be a secret, would it? Oh, and Hannah is **PRETTY**, I guess. Not that I notice such things. Like the old saying goes, **UGLINESS** is in the eye of the beholder!

STRENGTHS: Hannah's **MYSTERY** makes her hard to figure out. Where does she come from? Why do she and her father move around so much? I have a pretty good idea, but I'm not giving you any hints. You've got to figure **SOME** things out for yourself! Or you could just see the *Goosebumps* movie, if you haven't already. Oh, you **HAVE** seen it? Well, see it **AGAIN**. You know you want more of me!

WEAKNESSES: Hannah has a crush on Zach. If only it were the kind of crush that a **STEAMROLLER** does! I'd love to see Zach as flat as a **PANCAKE**! She also loves her weird old dad, R.L. Stine, even though he keeps her hidden away. Hey, that reminds me of **ME**! Stine always kept me packed away in a trunk. What's **WITH** that guy, anyway? Now do you see why I'm so eager to get my **REVENGE**?

BEST REVENGE: Feed Hannah to the **WEREWOLF** of Fever Swamp. Or sic a **VAMPIRE POODLE** on her! Better yet, let the **LAWN GNOMES** bury her in the backyard!

CHAMP

FIRST NAME: Champion (last name not known, but who cares anyway!)

DESCRIPTION: Champ is Zach's **SIDEKICK**. He's a nerd and a wimp, although I guess he's heroic in his own twisted way. Heroism—it's way **OVERRATED**! Before Zach came to town, Champ was the biggest **CHUMP** at Madison High School. Now he's part of Zach's group of do-gooders. Don't make me barf! (Really, you **DON'T** want to make me barf. It smells like rancid maple syrup!)

STRENGTHS: Champ is smarter than he looks. At least I hope he is, otherwise he wouldn't have enough **BRAIN CELLS** to keep breathing! He'd do anything for Zach, which makes him a dangerous **FOE**. Don't underestimate Champ. All those years of being picked on, bullied, and laughed at have given him character. Not as much as I **HAVE**, but still! He'll grow on you. Kind of like **FUNGUS**.

WEAKNESSES: "Champ" is short for "Champion," but his name is a **JOKE**. He's not a **CHAMPION** at all! If you can push him around, he might just run away. Or start **CRYING**! That's why it's so dangerous to have him around Zach and Hannah. When he's with them, he finds his hidden **COURAGE**.

BEST REVENGE: Cave trolls? They're too good for Champ. They'd probably spit him out! No, there's only one fitting revenge for this chump: **EVIL CLOWNS!** Send them in, and let them unleash their ghastly laughs!

MR. SHIVERS/ R.L. STINE

ALIASES: Fearly, Killroy, Ghoulberg, Papa

DESCRIPTION: The last of the **LOATHSOME FOURSOME** is the ringleader himself: R.L. Stine! Where does he come from? Where did he get his powers to write about monsters, creatures, aliens, and mutants and bring them to life? I have no idea! Even the World's Smartest Dummy has his limitations! All I know is this: I want my **REVENGE** against this **BOZO** with the nerd glasses and the bad taste in suits!

STRENGTHS: Stine is proud, powerful, and **HARD TO TRICK**. He also knows more than most schlubs who look like they've been living under a rock for a hundred years. He's a know-it-all, literally! So be careful. He may seem **MEEK**, but he's a mighty **GEEK**!

ME AND MY BELOVED PAPA!

WEAKNESSES: Luckily for us, Stine is not a friendly guy. He's downright **EERIE** and **WEIRD**! Zach has a hard time warming up to him, and even Hannah has her doubts. So it's not impossible to get him alone and weak! I want Papa to be **SHIVERING** with fright!

BEST REVENGE: Stine created all the monsters that I've talked about already, so you have to be careful. He's powerful—that is, for a total **SCHLUB**! Your best bet is to **TRAP** him inside one of his own magic books. Or **CRAM** him in a trunk. Turn him into a dummy like me! Only less smart and not evil at all, of course. When it comes to **DIABOLICAL**, no dummy can touch me!

WICKED QUIZZES

Nothing's eviler than pop quizzes—so here's one of my own! But don't sweat it, my gruesome servant. These questions aren't going to break your brain! They're strictly for fun. If you happen to SCARE up a little extra **EVIL** by answering them, though, I won't complain! Evil is the name of the game. (That, and **REVENGE**, of course!)

Which of my ghoulish monsters are you at heart (that is, if you even have a heart)? Take this **quiz** to find out!

What's your favorite horrendous place?

A) A nice green lawn

B) A graveyard, of course

C) A nice crypt

D) Any place with central air-conditioning

E) A creepy cave

Which monster would you pick as your sinister sidekick?

A) An evil dummy (just sayin'!)

B) A zombie

C) A vampire

D) A bug-eyed alien

E) A witch doctor

Your favorite food is . . .

A) Grass

B) Human flesh

C) Human blood

D) Anything from a vending machine . . . including the machine itself

E) Human bones—they're so deliciously crunchy!

What's your weapon of choice?

A) Throwing knives

B) Clawing hands that rip through the earth

C) Fangs

D) Snowball

E) Green mucus

What's your favorite Goosebumps book?

A) *Revenge of the Lawn Gnomes*

B) *Attack of the Graveyard Ghouls*

C) *Please Don't Feed the Vampire!*

D) *Beware, the Snowman*

E) *A Shocker on Shock Street*

Congratulations, my hokey little henchman! You fit right in with the rest of my lackeys.

Mostly A's

YOU ARE A LAWN GNOME! You might look nice and jolly on the outside, but everyone better stay off your grass . . . **OR ELSE!**

Mostly B's

YOU ARE A GRAVEYARD GHOUL! You love chilly green mists; dark, stormy nights; and stealing human bodies.

Mostly C's

YOU ARE FIFI THE VAMPIRE DOG! You love taking humans for walks, snarling, and nice bowls of warm blood. Mmm, delicious!

Mostly D's

YOU ARE THE ABOMINABLE SNOWMAN OF PASADENA! You've got a chilly temper and a big ol' sweet tooth.

Mostly E's

YOU ARE A GIANT PRAYING MANTIS! You like to play with your food before you eat it. And what you don't like, you spit out.

RIDDLE ME THIS

You didn't think you'd get to the end of this book without running across some bad riddles, did you? Here are a few of my most **GROAN-WORTHY**!

Q: WHY DID THE RAZOR-BEAKED CHICKEN CROSS THE ROAD?

A: TO **PECK** OUT YOUR EYES!

Q: WHY DID THE ROBOT EAT A LAMP?

A: BECAUSE HE PREFERRED A **LIGHT** LUNCH!

Q: HOW DO YOU KNOW
WHEN A VAMPIRE
IS SICK?

A: WHEN SHE'S **COFFIN**!

Q: WHAT IS A PIRATE'S LEAST
FAVORITE CHORE?

A: *YARRRRRRRR-D*
WORK!

Q: WHAT DID SLAPPY SAY WHEN HE CAME TO CLASS WITHOUT HIS HOMEWORK?

A: MY WEREWOLF ATE IT!

Q: WHAT'S A MUMMY'S FAVORITE KIND OF MUSIC?

A: WRAP!

Q: WHAT DO ZOMBIES WEAR TO STAY DRY WHEN THEY'RE DEVOURING PEOPLE?

A: THEIR BRAINCOATS!

Q: WHAT DID THE HEADLESS HORSEMAN SAY WHEN THE POLICE OFFICER PULLED HIM OVER FOR SPEEDING?

A: NOTHING. HE DOESN'T HAVE A MOUTH!

Q: WHY ARE INVISIBLE BOYS SUCH LOUSY LIARS?

A: BECAUSE YOU CAN SEE RIGHT THROUGH THEM!

THE END IS NEAR!

Okay, kiddos, let's recap! You've read the Slappy's Revenge mission statement—basically, this **entire** book! That means you know the rules of Trick Club. You also have an alias. And as an Agent of B.A.A.A.A.D., you've learned the Pledge of B.A.A.A.A.D.-llegiance by heart!

You know how to text Slappy-approved acronyms. You know how to make your own squad of monsters, how to eat like a **sicko**, and how to keep in **creepy** shape. You've learned how to make it through Mrs. Maaargh's class without getting eaten. You've memorized the Ick Files on our repulsive goody-goody foes! You've been schooled in the ways of **REVENGE**!

In short, you've learned all the **Twisted Tricks** from the World's Smartest Dummy! So what should we do first? Terrorize the locals? Destroy the town? Let's get silly!

Wait. What's that? It looks like . . . a van. A moving van! I almost forgot: I'm still in this basement! R.L. Stine's basement! And now the movers are coming down the stairs. Stine must be **MOVING** again!

Oh, no. That means . . .

Hey! Get your greasy mitts **OFF** of me, you big lug! **No!** Don't put me back in there! I'm **SLAPPY**! Ol' Crazy Eyes! Mr. Badboy! No? Not ringing any bells? How about The B.A.A.A.A.D. Boy? The Dummy That Is No Dummy? The World's Smartest Dummy? Um, Smiley?

Looks like your evil master Slappy is getting stuck back in the box. Help me, okay? Don't let them do this! I'll be crammed in this stinking case for **WHO KNOWS** how long? How am I supposed to get my revenge from IN HERE?

Why aren't you helping? Why are just **STARING** at me? Wait! Are you **LAUGHING**?! You'd better not be. No one laughs at SLAPPY! **NO ONE!**

So that's how it's gonna be, huh? You're on ZACH's side, aren't you? And Hannah's and Champ's and Stine's! I knew it. **BETRAYED!**

I'll remember this, you booger-brained moron! It may take a long time, even years, for me to get out of this case. But someday . . . **I WILL**! You can bet on it! And when I do, I'll have a new name to add to my Ick Files! A new ENEMY to get REVENGE on: **YOU**!

Until then, sleep tight, kiddos. And remember: Sometimes nightmares really **DO** come true! Or my name's not **SLAPPY**!

HA-HA-HA-HA!

SEE YOU IN YOUR SCREAMS!